She was clever and kind and she loved to read.

Everybody called her 'Beauty'.

But one day their luck changed. Their fine house was destroyed in a fire.

Then they heard that their trading ship had been wrecked at sea.

Beauty and her father had to move to an old cottage in the middle of a deep, dark forest.

Beauty had to work hard to make
the cottage a nice place to live.

But she was brave
and cheerful and she
set to work.

One day her father set off to sell some of the food they had grown. He asked Beauty what she would like him to get her from town.

"Just a rose please, Dad," Beauty replied.

On his way home, Beauty's father was caught in a terrible storm. He was soon lost in the forest.

As night fell he came to an old castle.

CRASH!

The door was open, but no one was at home. He crept inside and went to sleep.

In the morning Beauty's father went into the garden to pick a rose for his daughter.

"THIEF!" roared a voice.

From out of a shadow stepped... a beast.

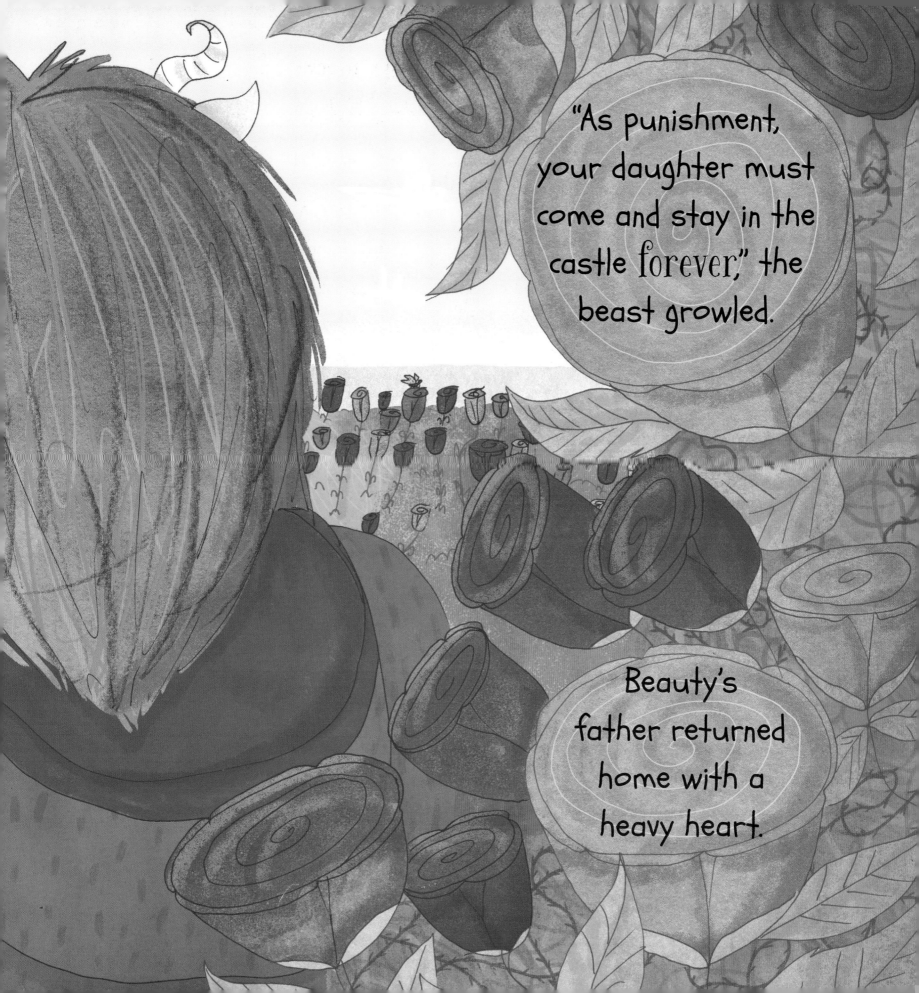

Beauty was sad and a bit scared, but she tried to make the best of it.

"It will be such an adventure, Dad," she said. She set off at once.

When she arrived at the castle, Beauty decided to explore. She saw a door marked 'Beauty's room'.

Inside was a lovely soft bed, and shelf after shelf of books! Perhaps the castle's owner might not be as cruel as he seemed.

That evening Beauty found a
delicious meal waiting for her
in the dining room. As she ate
the last bite, the beast
entered the room.

Though she was afraid, Beauty said thank you for her lovely room, and the books.

The beast looked pleased, and told her that everything in the castle was hers to do with as she wished.

Many weeks passed. Beauty spent her days reading.

Sometimes she walked in the gardens, and the beast would join her.

They ate dinner together each night. Beauty enjoyed talking to the beast, and looked forward to seeing him.

But she still missed her father terribly.

One day Beauty told the beast that she was worried about her father.

The beast gave her a magic mirror.

The mirror showed Beauty her father. He looked lonely and frail.

The beast agreed Beauty should go and look after him for a week.

"I've missed you so much!"

Beauty's father was overjoyed to see her.

At the end of the week, Beauty's father begged her to stay a little longer.

Beauty agreed, but that night she had a strange, sad dream.

She saw the Beast lying still in the castle gardens.

Somehow she knew he was dying. She felt like her heart was breaking.

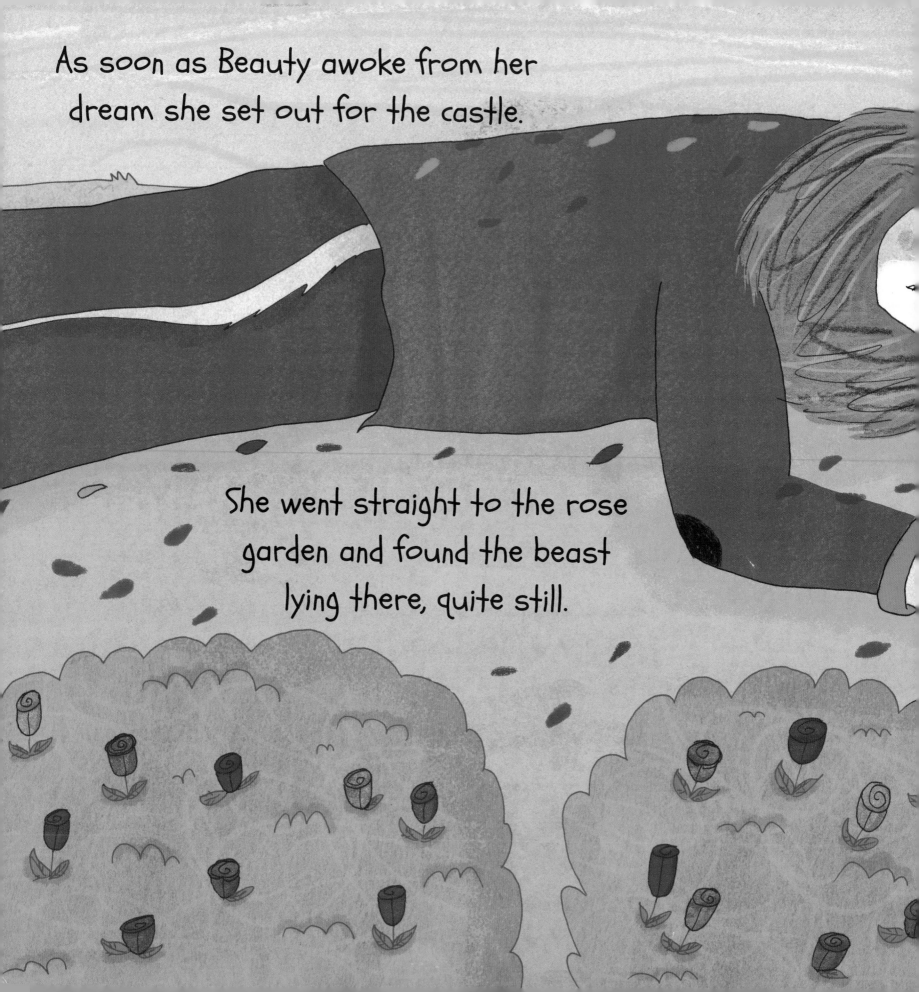

As soon as Beauty awoke from her dream she set out for the castle.

She went straight to the rose garden and found the beast lying there, quite still.

The beast whispered, "I thought you had forgotten me. Now I have seen you, I can die happy."

"No!" Beauty cried. "Don't leave me!"

"I love you."

At these words the beast vanished...
And a prince appeared in his place!

He had been cursed to be a beast
until someone could look beyond his
appearance and fall in love with him.

Hooray!

The two were happy together
for the rest of their days.